4.0/.5
19604

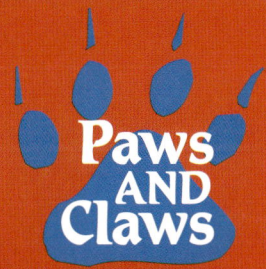

EAGLES

Sara Swan Miller

Paws AND Claws

PowerKiDS press
New York

For Lani
Be strong like them

Published in 2008 by The Rosen Publishing Group, Inc.
29 East 21st Street, New York, NY 10010

Copyright © 2008 by The Rosen Publishing Group, Inc.

All rights reserved. No part of this book may be reproduced in any form without permission in writing from the publisher, except by a reviewer.

First Edition

Editor: Amelie von Zumbusch
Book Design: Julio Gil
Photo Researcher: Nicole Pristash

Photo Credits: Cover © Tom Walker/Getty Images; p. 5, 7, 9, 13, 17, 19, 21 Shutterstock.com; p. 11 © istockphoto.com/Frank Leung; p. 15 © Clyde H. Smith/Peter Arnold, Inc.

Library of Congress Cataloging-in-Publication Data

Miller, Sara Swan.
 Eagles / Sara Swan Miller. — 1st ed.
    p. cm. — (Paws and claws)
 Includes index.
 ISBN 978-1-4042-4163-3 (library binding)
 1. Eagles—Juvenile literature. I. Title.
 QL696.F32M55 2008
 598.9'42—dc22
                                       2007019962

Manufactured in the United States of America

Contents

What Is an Eagle?	4
Built for Hunting	6
Strong Legs, Strong Claws	8
The Hunt	10
Giant Nests	12
Fuzzy Eaglets	14
Bold Bald Eagles	16
Beautiful Golden Eagles	18
Eagles in Trouble	20
Saving Eagles	22
Glossary	23
Index	24
Web Sites	24

What Is an Eagle?

Eagles are very large hunting birds. They are even bigger than their relatives the hawks. The biggest eagle is more than 6 feet (2 m) from wing tip to wing tip!

There are 59 different **species**, or types, of eagles. They live almost everywhere in the world. The only place they cannot live is in cold Antarctica. People break eagles into four groups. Sea eagles hunt fish. Booted eagles have feathers on their legs that look like boots. Snake eagles live mostly in Africa and eat snakes as well as other animals. The biggest eagles are the giant forest eagles.

This eagle is a bald eagle. Bald eagles are a species of sea eagle.

5

Built for Hunting

Eagles have wide wings. An eagle's wings and most of its body are covered in feathers. Most eagles have brown or gray feathers. **Female** eagles are larger than **males**. Both males and females are strong and have big heads. Their bills are large and **hooked**. An eagle uses its sharp bill to rip pieces of meat from its **prey**.

Eagles have **hooded** eyes that block out some of the Sun's brightness. Their **pupils** are very large. All eagles have very good eyesight. A flying eagle can spot a rabbit hiding on the ground from 1 mile (2 km) away!

Eagles, such as this African fish eagle, use their bills to breathe as well as to tear up and eat food.

Strong Legs, Strong Claws

All birds of prey, or hunting birds, have big, sharp claws, but an eagle's claws are extra big and sharp. These claws are called talons. They curve in and help an eagle hold on to its prey. When an eagle spots its prey, it dives down and catches the prey in its talons. Eagle talons are strong. For example, they let sea eagles catch and hold on to the slipperiest fish.

Eagles have strong legs, too. Giant forest eagles can pull large animals, such as monkeys and **sloths**, out of trees. These eagles' strong legs help them carry their heavy prey.

This Steller's sea eagle has such strong legs and talons that it can catch and carry off a young seal.

The Hunt

Like most birds, eagles do not have a very strong sense of smell. They find their prey by flying overhead and searching with their sharp eyes. When an eagle spots its prey far below, it dives down with its talons reaching out. It kills its prey by catching it in its talons. Most eagles fly away to a branch with their catch to eat it. A few eagles just eat their prey on the ground.

Eagles hunt all kinds of animals. Many eagles eat mice, rabbits, snakes, and birds. Others eat mostly fish and other water animals.

Fish eagles often catch fish by diving down and pulling the fish right out of the water.

Giant Nests

Eagles like to live mostly in mountains or forests. They build huge nests for their eggs in trees or on high cliffs. The nests are called **aeries**. A pair of eagles starts building an aerie by making a pile of heavy sticks. Then the eagles line the nest with soft grass. Most eagles keep adding new sticks to the same nest each year. An aerie may grow to 10 feet (3 m) across!

Most eagles **mate** for life. They do not like having other eagles around. If a stranger comes too close to the aerie, they will drive it away.

Eagle aeries are among the world's largest bird nests.
It takes eagles several weeks to build an aerie.

13

Fuzzy Eaglets

A female eagle lays one to three eggs in her nest. She sits on the eggs for about a month, until they **hatch**. Newly hatched eaglets, or baby eagles, are covered with soft fuzz. They are hungry and begin to eat just an hour after they hatch. The eaglets' father brings pieces of food to the nest, and the mother feeds them.

After about a month, the eaglets are almost fully grown. They hop about and wave their wings to make them strong. Their mother and father keep feeding young eagles for a few more weeks. Then the young start to hunt on their own.

Newborn eaglets crawl around their nest. Eaglets cannot stand or walk until they are several weeks old.

Bold Bald Eagles

Bald eagles are the best-known species of eagle. These eagles are not really bald. Their white-feathered heads just make them look that way. In 1782, the Founding Fathers chose the bald eagle as the national bird of the United States. They did so because it seemed brave and free. Look on the back of a dollar bill. Can you find a picture of a bald eagle?

Bald eagles live only in North America. They hunt near lakes and rivers. They eat mostly fish, but they also eat other small animals. Ducks, turtles, snakes, and rabbits all make a fine feast for a bald eagle.

Bald eagles get white heads and tails when they are about five years old.

Beautiful Golden Eagles

Golden eagles are a species of booted eagle. Golden eagles have feathered legs instead of bare ones like most other eagles. They are large, mostly brown eagles. Their necks and heads are covered with beautiful golden feathers. This is how they get their name.

Golden eagles once lived in many parts of the world. Now there are far fewer golden eagles. These remaining golden eagles live mostly in the mountains. They hunt for rabbits, mice, foxes, and deer. Golden eagles hunt in pairs. One eagle drives the prey to where the other is waiting to catch the prey with its talons.

Golden eagles live in parts of North America, Europe, Asia, and northern Africa.

19

Eagles in Trouble

Most people like eagles. Many countries, such as Mexico, the United States, and the Philippines, chose eagles as their national bird. Yet many species of eagles are in trouble and may disappear forever. Bald eagles and golden eagles have become uncommon in the United States. In South America, giant forest eagles called harpy eagles are disappearing.

People caused many problems for eagles. **Ranchers** killed eagles because they feared eagles would kill their sheep and cows. Farmers sprayed a **chemical** called DDT on crops. DDT got into some eagles' bodies. These eagles' eggs had thin shells and broke before they hatched.

Harpy eagles are one of the biggest kinds of eagles. These eagles eat mostly animals that live in the treetops.

21

Saving Eagles

In many parts of the world, people are trying to save eagles. In America, for example, DDT is now illegal. Killing an eagle is also now illegal in America and in many other countries. Now some eagles are beginning to make a comeback.

Another way to help eagles is to bring them back to places where they used to live. For example, people have brought 46 golden eagles into Ireland's Glenveagh National Park, where they had not been seen for 100 years. Let us hope that eagles around the world can be saved, thanks to the hard work of eagle lovers.

Glossary

aeries (EHR-eez) Nests of birds on a cliff or a mountaintop.

chemical (KEH-mih-kul) Matter that can be mixed with other matter to cause changes.

female (FEE-mayl) Having to do with women and girls.

hatch (HACH) To come out of an egg.

hooded (HU-ded) Shaded by a cover.

hooked (HUKT) Curled in at one end.

males (MAYLZ) Men and boys.

mate (MAYT) To be a pair for making babies.

prey (PRAY) An animal that is hunted by another animal for food.

pupils (PYOO-pulz) Openings in the eyes that change size to let the right amount of light into the eye.

ranchers (RANCH-erz) People who raise cattle, horses, or sheep on a farm.

sloths (SLOTHS) Slow-moving animals that live in trees and hang upside down.

species (SPEE-sheez) One kind of living thing. All people are one species.

Index

A
aerie(s), 12
Africa, 4

B
bald eagle(s), 16, 20
bill(s), 6
booted eagle(s), 4, 18

D
DDT, 20, 22

E
eggs, 12, 14, 20

eyes, 6, 10

F
feather(s), 4, 6, 18

G
giant forest eagle(s), 4, 8, 20
golden eagle(s), 18, 20, 22

P
prey, 6, 8, 10, 18
pupils, 6

S
sea eagle(s), 4
snake eagles, 4
species, 4, 18

T
talons, 8, 10, 18

W
wing(s), 4, 6, 14

Web Sites

Due to the changing nature of Internet links, PowerKids Press has developed an online list of Web sites related to the subject of this book. This site is updated regularly. Please use this link to access the list:
www.powerkidslinks.com/paws/eagles/

PROPERTY OF
MIDLAND VALLEY
CHRISTIAN ACADEMY
LIBRARY
594-9945